THE NURSERY VILLAGE

PEAR · TREE · FARM

Mary had a little lamb
Whose fleece was white as snow;
And everywhere that Mary went
The lamb was sure to go.

COLIN AND MOIRA MACLEAN

Kingfisher Books

Mother's cow was sleek and brown
  And Father's pig was pink.
Brother Johnny had a cat
  Whose coat was black as ink.

Sister Susie's hen was red
  And Baby's frog was green.
But Mary's lamb was white as snow
  And always sparkling clean.

Now everywhere that Mary went
Her lamb was close behind.
But one fine day he wandered off
To see what he could find.

He stole a carrot at the fair
And then knocked down some eggs.
When people shouted angrily
He tangled up their legs.

The naughty lamb ran up the lane
And disappeared from sight.
He strayed into the Big Dark Wood
Where all was black as night.

At last he saw a little house,
    Its windows shuttered tight.
Its chimney smoked and from its door
    There glowed a ghostly light.

The lamb crept in, a little scared,
And gazed around in awe;
Rats and bats and books of spells
And bubbling pots he saw.

A shadow crept along the wall –
It was a scrawny cat;
Behind the cat, an ugly witch
With broomstick and a hat.

The lamb took fright, he had to hide
    In case she cast a spell.
He leaped inside a bubbling pot –
    PLOP! (What a horrid smell . . .)

The lamb stayed quietly in the pot
    Until he heard a snore.
The witch was dozing by the fire . . .

The lamb made for the door!

I must find Mary, thought the lamb
Now running very fast.

Back through the trees and down the lane . . .
He reached the school at last.

He stumbled into Mary's class
To tell her where he'd been.
The children stared, the children laughed
Because the lamb was GREEN!

But Mary knew her little lamb
Although his wool was green.
"You naughty lamb, to run away!
Wherever have you been?"

The teacher smiled, "You know the rule:
No lambs allowed in class."
The little lamb went out to wait . . .

The bell rang out, at last!

Then, as he followed Mary home,
   The lamb saw Jack and Jill.
He gave a "Baa!" They jumped with fright
   And tumbled down the hill.

Their water spilled, the lamb was soaked,
   His wool was drenched and clean.
Though wet and cold, he skipped about;
   He was no longer green!

How glad he was when he reached home,
And what a welcome too:
The pig said "OINK!" The frog said "CROAK!"
And Mother's cow went "MOO!"

Then Mary hugged her little lamb
Whose fleece was white as snow.
Now everywhere that Mary goes
The lamb is *sure* to go.

To Nicola, Gilean and Fergus

Kingfisher Books, Grisewood & Dempsey Ltd,
Elsley House, 24–30 Great Titchfield Street,
London W1P 7AD

First published in paperback in 1992 by Kingfisher Books
10 9 8 7 6 5 4 3 2 1
Originally published in 1989 by Kingfisher Books

BRITISH LIBRARY CATALOGUING-IN-PUBLICATION DATA
A catalogue record for this book is available
from the British Library

ISBN 0 86272 900 9

Design by Pinpoint Design Company
Phototypeset by Waveney Typesetters, Norwich
Colour separations by Scantrans Pte Ltd, Singapore
Printed in Spain